DATE DUE

SEP 2 2 1998	

DEMCO, INC. 38-2931

DINOSTORY

by Michaela Morgan
pictures by True Kelley

DUTTON CHILDREN'S BOOKS · NEW YORK

Published in the United States by Dutton Children's Books,
a division of Penguin Books USA Inc.
Designer: Susan Phillips
Printed in Hong Kong by South China Printing Co.
First Edition   10 9 8 7 6 5 4 3 2 1

Library of Congress Cataloging-in-Publication Data

Morgan, Michaela.
    Dinostory/by Michaela Morgan; illustrated by
True Kelley.—1st ed.
        p.   cm.
    Summary: Andrew asks for a real live dinosaur for his
birthday and gets a lot more than he expected.
    ISBN 0-525-44726-1
    [1. Dinosaurs—Fiction. 2. Birthdays—Fiction.]
I. Kelley, True, ill. II. Title.
PZ7.M8255Di 1991
[E]—dc20   90-44935 CIP AC

For Andrew,
and all the kids who have ever wanted
a real live dinosaur—M.M.

For Nicky and Ward Dilmore, Jr.
and for Steven Lindblom, my personal dinosaur expert,
and special thanks to Donna Brooks—T.K.

Are you crazy about dinosaurs? Andrew Gilmore is.
Just look at his room.

At his birthday party, he had dinosaur decorations, dinosaur cookies, and a dinosaur cake. Andrew and his friends played Pin the Horn on the Triceratops, and Andrew won. It was *his* party, after all.

But what he didn't have was a real dinosaur, even though he'd asked for one. He'd wished for one. He'd prayed for one.

His Grandma had given him a gerbil, but it wasn't the same.

He'd read all the stories—you know the ones.

A boy is walking past
a deserted chalk pit
and spots a wallowing
Brontosaurus.

Daddy!

A boy finds an egg, and
it hatches into...

a Brontosaurus.

A boy has a birthday cake,
cuts it, wishes,
and it turns into...

guess what?

Well, Andrew had wished and wished before he'd blown out his candles, and he'd made sure his wish had been polite and reasonable. He'd said any sort of dinosaur would do. It didn't have to be a Brontosaurus (or an Apatosaurus, as some people called it). A Stegosaurus, Brachiosaurus, or even an Iguanodon would be quite acceptable, thank you. He'd opened his eyes, and what had he seen?

A sponge cake.

And as for finding a stray dinosaur lying around in a chalk pit! Life as Andrew knew it was just not like that. He couldn't even find a chalk pit. He didn't even know what a chalk pit was. Do you? Andrew did look in every deep hole he passed—just in case.

What he usually found was a workman, digging.

What the workman usually said was, "Beat it, kid, before you fall in."

So, all in all, it was just as well that Andrew knew a wizard.

"What would you like for your birthday, this time?" asked the wizard.

"I'd like to go back to prehistoric times, please," said Andrew, politely but firmly. "I want to meet a dinosaur."

"Back to prehistoric times!" cried the wizard. "Oh dear me, no. You're much too young to manage there all by yourself. Just think—there would be no Mom to make your snacks. No friends to play with. No Dad to wash behind your ears."

"I think I could manage without Dad to wash behind my ears," said Andrew.

"No, no, NO, Andrew. It's far too dangerous back there. What would I tell your Mom if you were trampled by a Tyrannosaurus . . . sat on by a Stegosaurus . . . damaged by a Diplodocus? Wouldn't you like a nice coloring book instead?"

But Andrew had millions of coloring books already, and most of them were dinosaur coloring books.

"Hmm...I suppose I could bring a dinosaur to *you*," muttered the wizard. "If I can think up a spell. Er...hocus-pocus—yes, that will do."

Hocus-Pocus Diplodocus
Or Tyrannosaurus Rex.
An Iguanodon might be fun.
OBEY the WIZARD'S HEX!
Protoceratops or Triceratops—
They're all the tops with us.
A Gorgosaurus could be gorgeous—
If it didn't make a fuss.
Anatosaurus, Apatosaurus—
Anything would do.
A Megalosaurus might add to the Chorus—
Or should I say, the ZOO!
Hadrosaur,
Stegosaur,
a Pterosaur
—or two?
A few...

"Stop! STOP!" cried Andrew. "Listen!"

KERRUMP!

"Aha!" cried the wizard.
"The dinosaur has landed."

"Ah," said the wizard, less confidently. "Another one."

SPERLASH! BOOM!

"Oops!" said the wizard, who was beginning to understand what was happening.

"Yup," said Andrew. "You've gone too far. You've gotten carried away. You've asked for too many!"

In the town, there was panic. It was raining dinosaurs. People were running...yelling...screeching...screaming.

"Don't worry," Andrew advised. "Dinosaurs are mostly vegetarians."

But even vegetarians can cause problems. Especially vegetarians who weigh thirty tons and are taller than three-story buildings.

A gently grazing Brontosaurus had flattened the greengrocer's, and it had only gone in to browse. The rest of the herd were drifting through the town burping (quite quietly for the size of them) as they nibbled on parks and posters, leaves and leaflets, bananas and billboards.

A peacefully floating Brachiosaurus was causing some
confusion in the swimming pool. As for the Tyrannosaurus
...well, you can guess what he (or she) was up to. Raging
up and down the street with claws, jaws, and roars all
equally terrifying.

"Why, oh, why did you have to mention Tyrannosaurus
rex?" moaned Andrew. "Just look at it!"

The ground was shaking (and so were the people) as
the enormous beast thundered down Main Street with its
head higher than a house, its eyes bigger than your head,
and its teeth—oh, its teeth!—they were sharper than razors
and bigger than your boots.

"It seems to be looking for something," muttered the
wizard.

"It is," wailed Andrew. "It's looking for meat. Live
meat. Run for it!"

Even the slowest dinosaurs were getting the idea that it might be time to move on—quickly. It looked as if the town was either going to be torn apart by a Tyrannosaurus —or squashed flat by a stampede of startled dinosaurs.

But—and here's a bit of luck—this Tyrannosaurus was obviously the sort of dinosaur who didn't listen to its mom. Because what does your mother tell you (again and again)? She says, "Look where you're going! Watch your step!"

The Tyrannosaurus did neither of these things. So it didn't notice the enormous hole in the ground—a hole made by the landing of a particularly bulky Brachiosaurus. It didn't see the hole. It didn't step around the hole. It just fell right into it.

Another sort of dinosaur could have hauled itself out, but the strength of a Tyrannosaurus lies in its enormous legs, its fierce jaws, and its incredible teeth. Not in its silly little arms.

"Hey," said the wizard, "that hole looks to me as if it's made of chalk. Your dinosaurs have discovered a chalk pit!"

Andrew was pleased. At last he'd found a dinosaur in a chalk pit.

He'd also seen a dinosaur hatching out of an egg. Well, really he'd seen a dinosaur lying in the middle of a heap of broken eggs. The Stegosaurus in the supermarket had tended to break a few things as it went through.

"It's all turning out brilliantly," said Andrew. "Now we can really have fun!"

Of course, Andrew expected to play hide-and-seek with the dinosaurs. He expected to climb up their backs and slide down their necks just like the kids in all the other dinosaur books.

But the truth is, dinosaurs are not really all that good at games. For one thing, they're too stupid to understand the rules. For another, they are too interested in eating to care about anything else.

"A dinosaur is not an ideal pet," observed the wizard. "I think you're better off with the gerbil, after all."

Andrew was beginning to agree. And he was beginning to get a little worried. He wasn't quite sure, but he seemed to remember the wizard mentioning a Gorgosaurus in his spell.

Now, Gorgosaurus is a close relative of Tyrannosaurus and every bit as unfriendly. Andrew wasn't certain, but he thought he could hear something crashing around in the distance. He couldn't be absolutely positive, but it sounded as if it was coming through the town towards them.

"I think it's time all these dinosaurs went back home," he said quickly.

So Andrew marched up to the nearest, mildest dinosaurs and flung his arms around them to hug them. "You have to go now," he said. "Good-bye."

They, of course, completely ignored him and just went on eating, wallowing, or standing around looking puzzled.

Meanwhile, the crashing sounds were getting much louder and much nearer. And the wizard was having trouble with his spell.

Do you know how to reverse a spell? That's right, you just say it backwards. Easy! Or is it? Can you say all those dinosaurs' names backwards? Our wizard started off something like this:

Sucoh-Sucop Sucodolpid ro suruasomaryt ker na nodonaugi thgim eb nuf YEBO EHT S'DRAZIW XEH!

It must have been more or less right because, as he carried on, dinosaurs started disappearing. One minute a Triceratops would be standing around looking dim. The next minute—POOF!—it was gone, back to wherever it had come from. An especially loud POOF! came from just outside the park. The Gorgosaurus was good and gone. Phew!

Soon there was not a dinosaur left. But Andrew had other
large and threatening creatures to deal with. The grown-ups
were coming! Staggering through the debris, crawling out of
their hiding places, picking their way through the remains of
Main Street, they came towards him.

"Hey, you!" one of them shouted. "Stay where you are!"

Uh-oh, thought Andrew, here comes trouble! Are they
going to go crazy? Are they going to put the wizard in jail? Or
stop my allowance for the rest of my life?

Andrew wished that he too could find a deep hole to fall
into or that he could just disappear. He tried saying WERDNA
a couple of times, but he didn't go POOF! He stayed exactly
where he was—with the grown-ups getting closer and closer.

"I'd have a better chance with a Gorgosaurus," he moaned.

But you know grown-ups! Who can begin to understand them?
What happens if you break one little window or get crayon
on the wall of just one room? They go completely nuts. But when
they came up to Andrew standing in the middle of hundreds
of broken windows and walls that had been knocked down—
or eaten—what did they do?

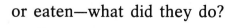

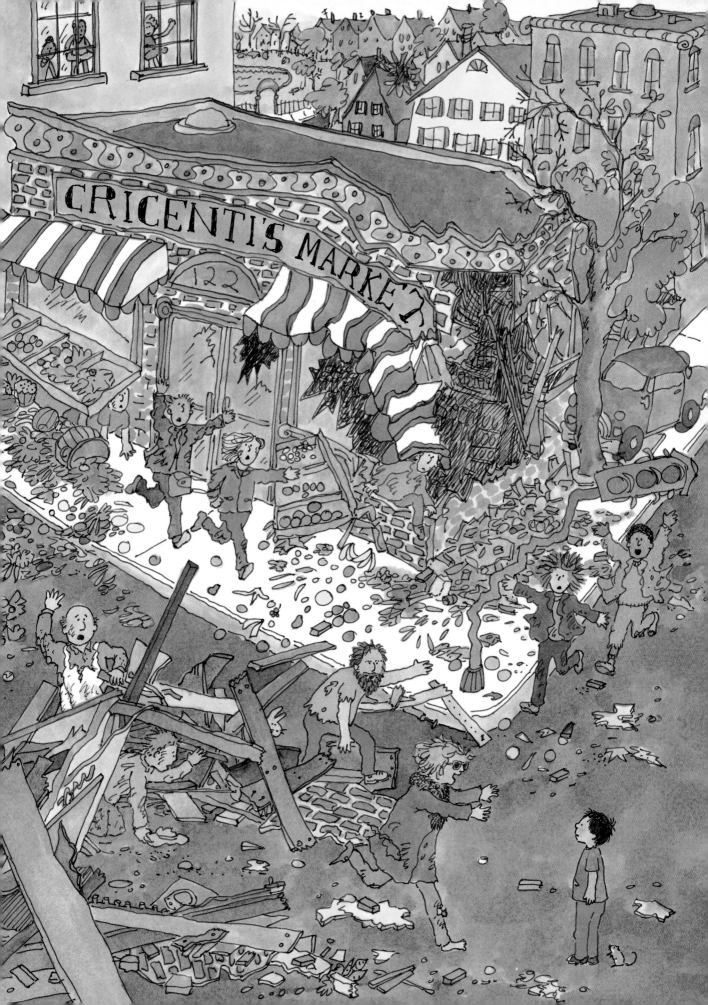

They shook his hand. They patted his back.
They hugged and *kissed* him. Yes, they did.
And what did they say?
They said, "Well done!"
"You've saved us!"
"The way you went up to those monsters and grabbed
hold of them and told them they had to go...."
"What nerve!"
"What courage!"
"What a hero!" they cried.
What luck! thought Andrew.

So, all in all, everything ended happily, just as it should.
But the wizard couldn't help saying, "I told you so. The
best place for a dinosaur is in its own time—or in a storybook.
A place for everything, and everything in its own place, eh?
You should have taken the coloring book, right, Andrew?
Andrew?"

But Andrew wasn't listening. He was too busy thinking
about what he could ask for on his next birthday.